Written by Dana Meachen Rau

Illustrated by Mike Cressy

Children's Press®
A Division of Grolier Publishing
New York • London • Hong Kong • Sydney
Danbury, Connecticut

For Charlie
—D.M.R.

To my one and only purple sister, Cookie
—M.C.

Reading Consultants
**Linda Cornwell**
Coordinator of School Quality and Professional Improvement
(Indiana State Teachers Association)

**Katharine A. Kane**
Education Consultant
(Retired, San Diego County Office of Education
and San Diego State University)

Visit Children's Press® on the Internet at:
http://publishing.grolier.com

Library of Congress Cataloging-in-Publication Data
Rau, Dana Meachen.
    Purple is best/ written by Dana Meachen Rau; illustrated by Mike Cressy.
        p. cm. — (A Rookie reader)
    Summary: Sue's blue paint and Fred's red paint get mixed together and create
purple, the best color of all.
    ISBN 0-516-21638-4 (lib. bdg.)          0-516-27001-X (pbk.)
    [1. Purple—Fiction. 2. Color—Fiction. 3. Painting—Fiction.]
I. Cressy, Mike, ill. II. Title. III. Series.
PZ7.R193975Pu 1999
[E]—dc21
                                            98-53053
                                            CIP
                                            AC

**GROLIER**
PUBLISHING

4 5 6 7 8 9 10 R 08 07 06 05 04 03 02

Sue paints with blue.

3

4

Fred paints
with red.

Sue thinks blue is cool.

7

Fred thinks red is better.

"Try blue," says Sue.

10

"Try red," says Fred.

# Oops!

15

The paint
tips and crashes.

The paint
drips and splashes.

18

Blue mixes with red.

21

Red mixes with blue.

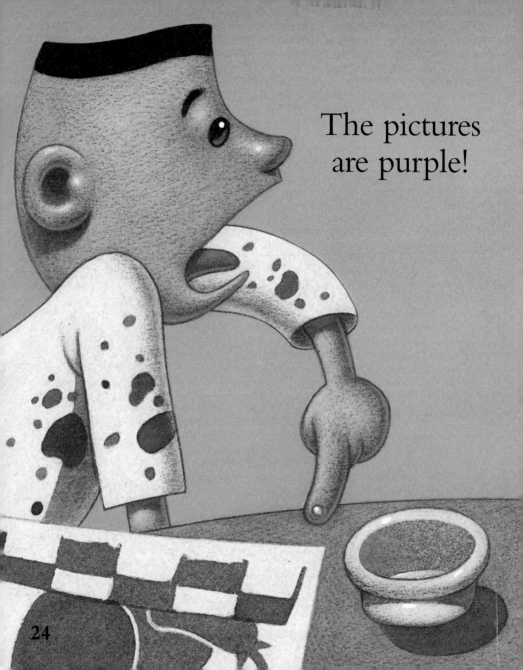

The pictures
are purple!

24

25

"Blue is cool," says Sue.

27

"Red is better,"
says Fred.

29

# "But purple...

is best!"

# WORD LIST (26 words)

| | | |
|---|---|---|
| and | Fred | says |
| are | is | splashes |
| best | mixes | Sue |
| better | oops | the |
| blue | paint | thinks |
| but | paints | tips |
| cool | pictures | try |
| crashes | purple | with |
| drips | red | |

## ABOUT THE AUTHOR

Dana Meachen Rau is the author of many books for children, including *A Box Can Be Many Things*, *The Secret Code*, and *Bob's Vacation* (which she also illustrated) in the Rookie Reader series. She has always studied both writing and art, and loves crafting words and pictures into the perfect story. She also works as a children's book editor and lives with her husband, Chris, and son, Charlie, in Farmington, Connecticut.

## ABOUT THE ILLUSTRATOR

Mike Cressy resides in the rainiest part of the United States—Washington State—paints pictures, and tries to stay warm and dry in his hovel, with the help of some hot cocoa.